Bantam Books in the Choose Your Own Adventure™ Series
Ask your bookseller for the books you have missed

THE THIRD PLANET FROM ALTAIR

BY EDWARD PACKARD

ILLUSTRATED BY PAUL GRANGER

BANTAM BOOKS

TORONTO · NEW YORK · LONDON · SYDNEY

RL5, IL age 10 and up

THE THIRD PLANET FROM ALTAIR
A Bantam Book / published by arrangement with
Harper & Row, Publishers, Inc.

PRINTING HISTORY
Lippincott edition published April 1979

A Selection of Junior Literary Guild

Bantam edition / November 1980
2nd printing ...... March 1981
3rd printing .... July 1981

Illustrated by Paul Granger
CHOOSE YOUR OWN ADVENTURE® is
a trademark of Bantam Books, Inc.

ISBN 0-553-13978-9

Published simultaneously in the United States and Canada

Bantam Books are published by Bantam Books, Inc. Its trademark, consisting of the words "Bantam Books" and the por-
trayal of a rooster, is Registered in U.S. Patent and Trademark
Office and in other countries. Marca Registrada. Bantam
Books, Inc., 666 Fifth Avenue, New York, New York 10103.

PRINTED IN THE UNITED STATES OF AMERICA

12 11 10 9 8 7 6 5 4

*To all those who would like to
travel faster than light.*

WARNING! ! ! !

Do not read this book straight through from beginning to end! These pages contain many different adventures you can have in outer space. From time to time as you read along, you will be asked to make a choice. Your choice may lead to success or disaster!

The adventures you take are a result of your choice. *You* are responsible because *you* choose! After you make your choice follow the instructions to see what happens to you next.

Remember—you cannot go back! Think carefully before you make a move! One mistake can be your last . . . or it *may* lead you to fame and fortune!

For many years, astronomers tried to detect messages from life in outer space. Finally, at an observatory on top of Mauna Kea in Hawaii, these signals were recorded:

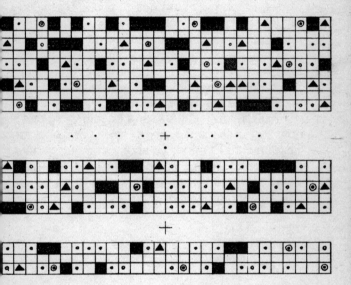

Their source was found to be the third planet from Altair, a yellow-white star sixteen light-years from Earth.

Scientists everywhere agreed that the signals, which were repeated continuously every few minutes, must certainly have been sent by intelligent beings—but they were unable to agree upon their meaning. . . .

Go on to the next page.

2

You are one of a crew of four aboard the spaceship *Aloha*. You and your companions have been chosen to journey to Altair to seek whomever, or whatever, is sending messages. You hope to travel the vast distance in only a few weeks, instead of hundreds of years, by making use of time-contraction technology. All systems operated perfectly as you blasted off and accelerated past Mars, Jupiter, and Saturn and on into interstellar space.

Now, two weeks later, you are standing on the bridge, watching the rearview display screen. The sun has diminished in size and brightness so that it now looks like an ordinary star. With you are Captain Bud Stanton, veteran astronaut; Professor Henry Pickens, cosmologist; and Dr. Nera Vivaldi, an anthropologist specializing in interspecies communication.

Turn to page 4.

Suddenly space around the ship is filled with flickering light. You glance at the captain. He is rigid, as if he were frozen. Sparks dance around the computer. Your body begins to tingle.

Pickens is leaning over the sensor-data display screen, shivering as though he had a severe chill. "We must be passing through an antimatter storm," he says in a shaky voice. "Fortunately, a mild one."

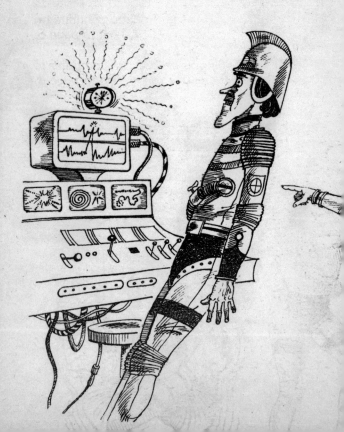

"Mild, perhaps," you reply, "but look at the captain! He looks paralyzed!"

"I think we should turn back," says Dr. Vivaldi. "We're not equipped to handle this, especially without the captain."

"I think we're through the worst of it," Pickens says. "I'm sure the captain would want us to continue on our mission."

Your decision will break the deadlock.

If you allow the Aloha *to continue on course to Altair, turn to page 6.*

If you instruct the computer to change your course, turn to page 8.

6

"Proceed; use hyperspeed evasion," you tell the computer. The *Aloha* shudders as it streaks through space. Pickens takes the captain to his cabin. You begin to feel normal again. The *Aloha* has passed safely through the storm, but signals from the Third Planet can no longer be detected.

"The captain will recover," Pickens informs you a short while later, "but I do not think we have seen our last antimatter storm."

The following days pass uneventfully. The sun-star Altair grows so bright that you can no longer look directly at it. You have already entered its solar system, and soon you approach the Third Planet—a blue-green sphere that looks a lot like Earth, except for the strangely symmetrical bands of white clouds orbiting the planet far above its surface. The Third Planet has three small moons, one of which, sensors report, is totally covered with water.

The water moon and the orbiting clouds are such unusual phenomena that you are inclined to investigate them before attempting to enter the planet's atmosphere.

If you investigate the water moon, turn to page 9.

If you investigate the clouds orbiting the planet, turn to page 10.

If you head directly for the Third Planet, turn to page 13.

As you continue on, you notice that what you had thought was a lake is actually a meadow of blue-gray moss. You are relieved to know that you are not losing your senses.

You cross the mossy meadow and approach a stream that is almost obscured by the thick underbrush along its banks. Near the stream you pass clumps of large, bushy plants waving in the wind. But there is something odd about this . . . there is no wind!

The plants seem to be searching for something—perhaps food. One of them is bending down over you! In a moment, you realize that you have been surrounded by the plants.

If you dive into the underbrush in the hope that the plants won't be able to get at you there, turn to page 46.

If you try to run away from the plants, turn to page 48.

You change course and begin to chart a more indirect route to Altair. The antimatter effects subside. All systems return to normal. The captain stirs as if awakening from a long nap.

"Are you all right, captain?" you ask.

He smiles at you, but there is a strange look in his eyes. "Set course for Deneb 5—ultrahype," he says in a monotone voice.

"But what about our mission?" you say.

"That is an order!"

"I sense an alien presence among us," Dr. Vivaldi says. "It must have lodged in the mind of the captain and be gaining strength. You must act."

*If you follow the captain's orders,
turn to page 12.*

*If you do not obey the captain,
turn to page 22.*

The *Aloha* changes course, approaches the water moon, and glides down through the heavy gray clouds that hide most of its surface. Suddenly you can see the ocean below. It is swept by enormous waves that look like snow-covered mountains and are constantly forming and collapsing.

"The winds are strong, and there is no land to stop the waves from building higher and higher," Pickens explains.

The captain returns to the bridge, apparently recovered. He takes one look at the waves and says, "Let's get out of here. Set course for the Third Planet."

The *Aloha* responds. Within a few hours you are looking down on a new world of blue oceans and green forests.

The computer reports that the atmosphere of the Third Planet is a lightweight, nontoxic gas—you will be able to breathe it just like the air on Earth. The captain asks you to embark in *Cygnet I,* one of the ship's two-seater space shuttles, to search for signs of intelligent life. You have the choice of taking with you Pickens, Dr. Vivaldi, or Bluenose, an underwater robot.

If you select Pickens, turn to page 14.

If you select Dr. Vivaldi, turn to page 15.

If you select Bluenose, turn to page 16.

As you are approaching the orbiting clouds, the captain returns to the bridge to reassume command. He seems to have recovered completely.

"These clouds fascinate me," he says. "They are so symmetrically shaped. It's almost as if they were placed there by intelligent beings—perhaps to protect space stations from ultraviolet radiation."

The *Aloha* cruises over the clouds and glides down through them. "Great heavens!" the captain exclaims. You marvel at the sight before you—a city in orbit, the buildings made of clearest crystal and connected by graceful ramps that soar over beautiful parks. Oddly, the city appears to be totally deserted.

"This may be where the signals were coming from," the captain says. "Will someone volunteer to explore the city while the rest of us survey the planet's surface from the *Aloha?*"

If you volunteer, turn to page 17.

If you do not, turn to page 19.

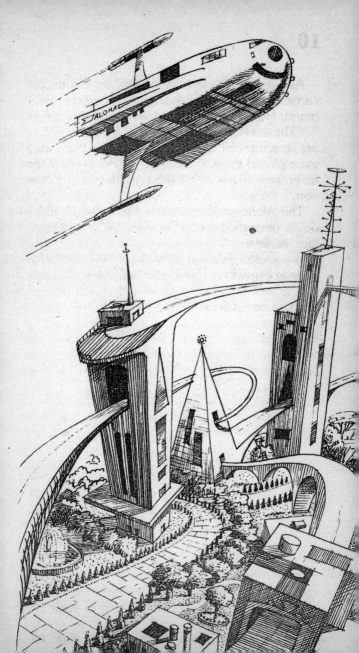

12

You carry out the captain's order, and the *Aloha* veers toward Deneb 5.

Suddenly, the ship shudders. Everyone is thrown about. The power goes off. Auxiliary lights flash on.

"DANGEROUS INCREASE OF X-RAY RADIATIONS ON THIS COURSE," the computer reports. "SAFE LEVELS NOW EXCEEDED."

"We must stay on course!" the captain barks.

"I'm sure the captain knows what he is doing," Pickens says.

Dr. Vivaldi takes you aside. "Now the alien force is controlling Pickens," she says.

If you continue to follow the captain's orders, turn to page 24.

If you challenge the captain, turn to page 25.

The *Aloha* passes through the uppermost levels of the Third Planet's atmosphere and glides into stationary orbit. The captain, who has now recovered, asks you to take a Cygnet shuttlecraft to the surface. You load up packs of instruments, food, and water. The Cygnet separates from the *Aloha*.

You bring the shuttlecraft down to a thousand meters above the ground, intending to look for unusual features. Almost at once, you are blinded by lights flashing all around you. You quickly make an emergency landing, setting down in a smooth meadow. You try to make contact with the *Aloha*, but radio communications have been cut off.

If you get out and explore, turn to page 20.

If you try to return to the Aloha, *turn to page 34.*

14

You and Pickens board the Cygnet, detach from the *Aloha,* and glide along a few hundred meters above the Third Planet's surface, following first the seacoast and then a river upstream toward its mountain source. Hospitable as the planet appears, you see no cities, roads, or other signs of civilization. You continue on, crossing a ridge of high mountains. Stretching before you is a vast expanse of desert.

"The mountains must catch the moisture-laden air blowing in from the sea, so rain rarely reaches the interior," Pickens says. "But there may be life here someplace. See those cliffs? If I'm right, they are made of limestone, and there may be large caves under them. If this planet has been threatened, societies may have formed in the caves. Perhaps we should land here and investigate."

If you land by the cliffs, turn to page 26.

If you fly on into the interior, turn to page 27.

You and Dr. Vivaldi detach from the *Aloha* in *Cygnet I,* glide down close to the Third Planet's surface, and follow a ridge of mountains. You look down on both sides, searching for signs of life.

"Wait," says Dr. Vivaldi, "this is exciting. The Cygnet's sensors report electronic emanations from those gray cliffs."

You land immediately on the ridge, and both of you climb out of the shuttlecraft. Nearby, you spot a trail leading to the base of a cliff. You follow it a short way and come upon the opening of a cave. You cautiously step inside. You are in a huge cavern that is dimly illuminated by amber light coming from some phosphorescent material on the walls.

Turn to page 101.

With Bluenose positioned for launching, you drop down to the surface of the Third Planet and cruise along the seacoast.

Soon you notice rippling water where two currents collide—an ideal place to look for sea life. You land the Cygnet on the surface of the ocean and lower Bluenose over the side. As the robot descends, you are startled to observe some large shadowy objects moving beneath the surface of the water.

Bluenose begins to wobble as it moves. One of its stabilizing units has malfunctioned. Your sensors report that a sudden electrical surge has burned out some circuits.

If you let Bluenose continue to explore, turn to page 30.

If you retrieve Bluenose and continue cruising along the coast, turn to page 33.

The *Aloha* hovers above the center of the city. You don your space suit, step out through a port, and float gently down to one of its supporting planes. You watch the *Aloha* glide away and then turn your attention to the city before you. The walkways and buildings are as clean and fresh looking as if they had been built yesterday. You wonder who lived here. Why did they leave? Where did they go?

There is very little gravity in the city, and you can almost fly along the streets. You enter a building and find furniture that looks as if it might have been designed for very small people. Another building is capped by hundreds of spires. Inside it, you find electronic equipment. Perhaps it is radio transmitting equipment and the spires are antennae. Could *this* be where the signals were coming from?

Go on to the next page.

18

The next building is shaped like a dome. Inside, the walls are covered with maps and charts of the galaxy. One chart in particular strikes your eye. It looks like this:

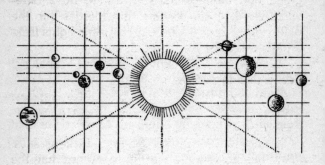

If you continue to explore the city, turn to page 28.

If you radio the Aloha at once to tell of your discovery, turn to page 32.

Since no one volunteers to explore the cloud city, the captain decides to proceed to stationary orbit. The *Aloha* gracefully peels off from the clouds and arcs closer to the surface of the Third Planet. You look down with fascination on a green and blue planet surrounded by a blue-white band of atmosphere that merges into the blackness of space. You can see eerie lights flickering around the planet's poles.

"Computer," the captain calls out, "analysis: beta radiation, screen 4."

In a few seconds the computer replies: "PHENOMENON UNKNOWN ON EARTH. HYPOTHESIS APPROACHING ANTIMATTER STORM."

"I think the computer's right," Pickens says. "And this storm will be far more intense than the one we experienced in space."

"We may have to get out of here at hyperspeed," the captain says, "but I want to find out as much as I can before we do. It's a dangerous situation, but we have a job to do. Someone is going to have to take *Cygnet I* down and check out the surface."

If you say you'll go, turn to page 35.

If you decline, turn to page 36.

In the distance is a large lake. Along its shores are groves of trees. You climb out of the shuttle-craft and walk toward the lake. As you get closer, you are amazed to see that what you took to be trees ahead of you look more like giant weeds or wild flowers.

Suddenly, there is nothing under your feet. You are sliding down a steep slope into a dark, smelly pit.

You are shaken but unhurt. As you catch your breath, you notice a tunnel leading into the pit. This could be an escape route.

Turn to page 38.

You begin your descent. For a time, the Third Planet's atmosphere is fairly calm—but then you find yourself crash-diving through what seem like hundreds of thunder and lightning storms. Visibility is zero in the driving hail and sleet. You begin to lose power. The presentation screen shows only a blurred, flickering image; your radar is out. The altimeter gauge is fluctuating wildly. A violent wind has carried you over the mountains. The temperature is dropping rapidly.

Suddenly, you feel a thump. Now there is nothing but blackness ahead. You decelerate rapidly to a stop. All is quiet.

To the rear you can see a long tunnel at the end of which is a gray disc—a patch of clouds. You are buried in deep snow. Your radio is burned out. But you have cold-weather gear and plenty of provisions. You can probably make your way up through the tunnel and out of the mountains. Your greatest fear is that you will never see another human being again.

The End

You point your mini-laser at the captain. "Since your conduct violates our orders, we are required to confine you," you tell him. You march the captain to his quarters and lock him in.

When you return to the bridge, you find that Dr. Vivaldi has already ordered an emergency change of course to get you away from the alien mind force.

Later, you go to the captain's quarters to check on his condition. You find him up and about, looking as if nothing had happened.

"You did the right thing in confining me," he says. "But I'm OK now. Let me out—that's an order!"

If you decide to let the captain resume command, turn to page 44.

If not, turn to page 45.

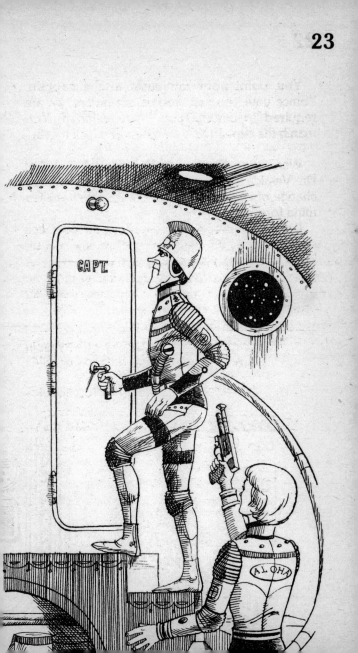

You follow the captain's orders. After all, he is still the captain. The *Aloha* vibrates frighteningly as it hurtles through space toward Deneb 5.

"Help!" the captain cries. As you watch, his body becomes transparent and vanishes. Then you feel *yourself* evaporating. You still sense your existence, yet you no longer have a body. You are now but a single cell in some great cosmic mind.

The End

You trust Dr. Vivaldi and feel sure that her perception of the situation is accurate.

Setting your mini-laser on "stun," you stand behind Pickens. As you touch the electronic trigger you whisper, "Advise the captain to hype out."

"You've freed me!" the captain shouts. "Quick, computer—hype reverse. Prepare for shock-turn in fifteen seconds!"

"It's still here," Dr. Vivaldi says, "But it can't act unless it's infecting someone. You broke its hold on the captain's mind when you stunned Pickens, but only temporarily."

"It's trying to get me again!" the captain gasps.

"We can *will* it out of our minds," Dr. Vivaldi says.

At that moment you are conscious of an overwhelming thought—that you will be happy if you surrender to the alien force, and will die if you do not surrender.

If you surrender, turn to page 42.

If you concentrate against the alien force, turn to page 43.

The Cygnet smoothly descends to the surface, and you cut the jets just as it touches down. But instead of landing on firm ground, the Cygnet slowly begins to sink into some soft, sticky substance.

"What have we landed in!" you ask.

"It looks like sandstone," Pickens says, "but it seems to be permeated with oil. I've never seen anything like this anywhere. And if we don't stop sinking within a few minutes, we're finished."

As he is talking, you pull the emergency ascent levers. Most of the jets have become clogged, but one of them fires a blast that tilts the Cygnet on its side.

"Now we'll go down faster!" Pickens says.

You instantly press the radio distress-call button. The Cygnet's computer calculates and radios your location.

Suddenly all is blackness outside. Pickens says, "There's hope of rescue if we don't sink much farther."

But you do.

The End

As you and Pickens fly across the desert, you see beneath you a dome about twelve meters high and twenty meters in diameter. You bring the Cygnet down to a landing and walk up to the dome. It is as blue as the sky, and made of a substance like the hardest crystal. At last you have evidence of intelligent life on the Third Planet.

"It appears," Pickens says, "that this is part of some large underground settlement. The only way to find out is to open it with a laser-beam cutter. I'm going to do it."

"But it may have a defense system," you point out.

"No need to worry," Pickens replies. "Our sensors would have detected their monitoring system."

If you agree to let Pickens cut open the crystal dome, turn to page 49.

If you insist on first reporting back to the Aloha, turn to page 50.

You continue on through the cloud city, marveling at the architecture of the buildings—and the clouds.

In a square in the center of the city is a complex array of electronic equipment. Among the multitude of lights, control knobs, and display screens is a console with a keyboard and what appear to be a microphone and speakers. You press the most prominent button on the keyboard. Immediately you hear a succession of musical tones, and then vocal sounds that remind you of a foreign language. The computer is talking to you!

Feeling somewhat awkward, you answer the computer, saying, "I come from the planet Earth."

Turn to page 79.

Several of the large objects are moving close to Bluenose. On your display screen, you can see the robot diving swiftly to escape them. Suddenly, your screen goes blank. A few minutes later Bluenose bobs up to the surface. When you pull it aboard, you find that every one of its circuits has been burned out.

Could Bluenose have been shocked by a huge electric fish? Or did it breach the defenses of some intelligent life form? The only way for you to find out is to descend to the ocean floor in your diving bubble.

The surface of the water is calm, but massive black clouds loom over the horizon, and strange flashes of pink light dance above the waves. This may not be a good time to leave the Cygnet.

If you dive, turn to page 41.

If you do not, turn to page 51.

You radio the captain and tell him about the chart. He is excited to hear of your discoveries in the cloud city, but advises you that the Third Planet may be overwhelmed by antimatter at any moment. You hastily take some photographs of the city before the *Aloha* arrives to pick you up. Soon you are again traveling through interstellar space.

You and the others study all the data.

"The records left by the inhabitants of the planet show that they studied the galaxy in an effort to find a new home," the captain writes in his official report. "The people who lived in the cloud city abandoned it because it is doomed. They have chosen as a refuge our own solar system."

Dr. Vivaldi remarks, "When we return to Earth, we may find the same beings we journeyed so far to meet, or—some day in the future—they may come to meet us."

The End

You retrieve Bluenose, and the Cygnet lifts off from the surface of the ocean. As you cruise along the coastline, you notice a huge crevice, as if an earthquake had opened a crack in the planet's crust. You veer toward it and then descend into a narrow canyon, the walls of which are tiers of bright, jagged rocks streaked with vivid reds and oranges.

Suddenly, sparks flash around your equipment. The Cygnet's electronic controls cease to function. You begin to plummet. You work your manual controls for emergency glide descent. The Cygnet's nose slowly tilts upward, and you glide down and through the canyon at frightening speed. Now only a narrowing ribbon of light from the sky illuminates the depths of the canyon. You see the ground coming up fast. You stall out at the right moment, land hard, and slide a couple of hundred meters.

Lights come on. Your electrical system is working again. You can hear signals on your radio— the same ones beamed to Earth from this planet! You realize that your quest has ended—and just begun.

The End

You take off immediately. As you streak through the stratosphere, you are startled to see that the whole sky is bathed in an orange, flickering glow. The Cygnet's small computer flashes danger signals.

The *Aloha* should be coming into view now—but it is gone!

The flickering light subsides, but you fear that it may soon flare up again.

If you decide to return to the surface of the Third Planet and seek refuge, turn to page 21.

If you decide to remain in orbit and wait for the Aloha, *turn to page 40.*

You volunteer to go down to the surface of the Third Planet. At the last minute, Dr. Vivaldi says she will come with you. The two of you board the Cygnet, cut loose from the *Aloha,* and glide down toward the planet's surface.

"Those cliffs offer natural protection from the wind and from the heat of Altair," Dr. Vivaldi says as you descend. "They also mark the boundary between desert and mountains. On Earth, places like this are natural sites for settlements."

You land and proceed on foot, following a trail along the base of the cliffs. The trail winds along a narrow ledge beside an overhanging wall of pinkish gray rock. Soon you come upon the opening to a large cave. The two of you enter the cave and cautiously make your way through a long chamber that is dimly illuminated by soft amber light coming from some phosphorescent material on the walls.

Turn to page 101.

You are very reluctant to go down to the surface of the Third Planet when an antimatter storm may be approaching. Pickens feels the same way. Dr. Vivaldi, however, says she will go.

"I'll come with you," the captain says.

The captain leaves you in charge of the *Aloha*. He and Dr. Vivaldi board a Cygnet shuttlecraft and leave for the surface of the Third Planet.

Soon afterward, Pickens joins you on the bridge. "This solar system is being bombarded by tiny particles of antimatter," he tells you. "If we run into a large concentration of them, they could destroy us!" As he is speaking, the sky becomes streaked with tongues of flickering light.

"WE HAVE LOST COMMUNICATION WITH CYGNET I," the computer reports. "ANTIMATTER ACTIVITY APPROACHING CRITICAL. SOLAR FLARE DANGER CRITICAL. RECOMMEND IMMEDIATE WITHDRAWAL TO OUTERMOST PLANET."

You cannot reach the captain by radio.

If you follow the computer's recommendation and leave, turn to page 54.

If you keep the Aloha in orbit and wait for the captain, turn to page 58.

Coming toward you out of the tunnel is an animal with the terrible face, quivering whiskers, and mean mouth of a rat—but this thing is the size of a bear, and its teeth are like those of a huge wolf.

As the rat beast comes closer, you reach for your laser pistol, but it is gone—lost during your slide into the pit. You quickly pick up a handful of sand; then, when the beast is almost upon you, you hurl the sand in its eyes and run past it to the tunnel.

The rat beast is apparently blinded or confused, for you are able to escape through the

tunnel, which winds upward to the surface of the planet.

Thankfully, you step out into the fresh air. But the lake is gone! Perhaps it was a mirage. It is not pleasant to think that your eyes may be playing tricks on you.

You feel exhausted from your ordeal, confused about where you are, and anxious to return to the *Aloha*.

If you start out immediately to find your way back to the Cygnet, turn to page 7.

If you sit and rest for a few moments, turn to page 59.

As you wait in stationary orbit, you are relieved to see a spaceship on your radar screen—but you are unable to make radio contact with it. Watching through the port, you are amazed to see a gleaming silver object approaching. It is not the *Aloha!* The alien vessel is shaped like a perfect cylinder. Though it is as big as a supertanker, it maneuvers like a helicopter. It slows, turns, and hovers near your tiny craft.

As you watch helplessly, a thirty-meter-long section of the ship slides back. You pull your emergency acceleration lever, but your circuits are dead. The Cygnet is drawn irresistibly into the huge spaceship, and the huge door closes silently behind you.

Suddenly, the compartment is brightly illuminated. Several four-legged creatures walk toward the Cygnet. They have a frightening appearance, but they are raising their antennae in what seems to be a gesture of friendship.

The End

You enter your diving bubble and descend rapidly into the ocean depths. Within a few moments your sensors report electrical charges. You can see oily blobs moving through the water. Farther down, a large and frightening-looking fish heads toward you. Suddenly it stops swimming and floats aimlessly—dead! The blobs encircle their victim and join into one huge blob, silently consuming the prey. Your sensors warn of other objects approaching.

You want to take back as full a report as possible on your ocean exploration, and you feel fairly safe with your laser weapon. On the other hand, the blobs are like nothing you've ever encountered on Earth or in space, and it may be more prudent to get away from them at once.

If you continue to explore, turn to page 53.

If you surface immediately and return to the Cygnet, turn to page 109.

You relax and hope that you will soon be happy. In a moment, Dr. Vivaldi collapses. You feel yourself drifting into another state of being. Your body is tingling; you can feel no other sensations. Now you are but a consciousness drifting through space, wondering what will become of you. You will not find out for billions of years.

The End

"Concentrate!" you call to the captain. "Fight the alien force! If we can all hold on for a few minutes, the *Aloha* will carry us out of its range."

The *Aloha* streaks away from Deneb 5.

"We're going to make it," Dr. Vivaldi whispers.

Pickens slowly gets up and rubs his head, a dazed look on his face. "I don't know where I've been," he says, "but I know there is another universe besides our own."

Astounded but grateful to have escaped from the mysterious force, you resume course to Altair. A week later, the ship enters Altair's planetary system. Pickens goes to report this news to the captain, who has been quite ill since his encounter with the alien mind force.

The *Aloha* nears the Third Planet. You and Dr. Vivaldi stand on the bridge marveling at the perfectly shaped clouds orbiting thousands of kilometers above the planet's surface. Soon Pickens returns and tells you that the captain is much improved and is excited to hear that the *Aloha* is about to reach its destination.

Turn to page 10.

When you and the captain return to the bridge, Dr. Vivaldi reports that audio sensors have picked up unusual sounds coming from Caprion, an area of space believed to be the origin of the primordial fireball—the place where the universe came into being.

"I recommend altering course to Caprion," Pickens says. "It is there that we may find the answer to the most important question of all time: how our universe came into existence."

"Yes," Dr. Vivaldi says, "I think our true destiny is in Caprion."

The captain turns to you. "I think we should try to get to Altair," he says, "but if you also think we should go to Caprion, that's what we'll do."

If you recommend resuming course to Altair, turn to page 61.

If you recommend diverting the ship toward Caprion, turn to page 64.

You say, "I'm sorry, captain, this is for your own good," and quickly lock the door of his cabin. Then you return to the bridge.

Abruptly the *Aloha* begins to tremble. The stars on the display screen whirl into new positions. "TIME WARP DISRUPTION! TIME WARP DISRUPTION!" says the computer.

"Full-range screen presentation!" you call out. The whole array of stars and galaxies appears.

"I can hardly believe it," Dr. Vivaldi says in an awed tone. "We know where we are, but we don't know *when* we exist. Earth may not yet have been born, or it may already have disappeared."

"We must activate the chronistan!" Pickens cries. "It is our only hope of returning to our own time."

"What if we fail?" you wonder aloud.

Pickens thinks a moment. "We might end up in a time from which we could never escape— possibly even a time before any matter existed in the universe. We would then be totally and finally alone."

The computer rates the probability of success at 32 percent. Dr. Vivaldi and Pickens say they will trust your judgment.

If you activate the chronistan, turn to page 55.

If you decide to remain in the present time, whatever it is, turn to page 60.

Hidden in the underbrush, you are safe from the moving plants, but you may have to stay hidden forever unless you can think of a way to elude the plants. Then, as the sun-star Altair drops behind the hills, the plants go limp. Apparently they can only move when energized by strong light and heat from their sun.

You waste no time in making your way onto high ground, hoping to get your bearings. Then you spot a familiar shape in the sky—a Cygnet shuttlecraft. You have lost your laser pistol, but you are able to signal the Cygnet by the primitive but effective method of building a fire.

The Cygnet disappears from view, but then circles back. It turns, banks, and in a few moments is on the ground beside you.

"Thank goodness I've found you," Pickens says. "You must be exhausted, and we should return to the *Aloha,* but first let me fly you a short way over the desert beyond those hills. I spotted something we should investigate."

Turn to page 27.

You start to run, but at once you feel something like a wet towel twining around your leg. You whirl about and slash at it with your knife. It loosens its grip, but another plant flaps against your face, its leaves curling around your neck. You duck, twist, and run as fast as you can. In a few minutes, you reach the safety of a forest of giant ferns.

Soon you see a blurry shape running toward you. A moment later, a band of humanoid creatures runs past. You wonder whether you should try to communicate with them—perhaps they could help you learn more about the Third Planet. On the other hand, they might hold you captive, or worse.

If you call out to them, turn to page 65.

If you stay hidden until they pass, turn to page 67.

Pickens aims his laser-beam cutter at the crystal dome. You watch in amazement as it fires away at full power for almost a minute without even scratching the surface. "This is like no material on Earth," Pickens remarks.

Finally, a thin trail of smoke begins to rise from the dome. The smoke thickens. Suddenly the whole surface of the dome is alive with flickering electric charges. You and Pickens leap back and run for the safety of the Cygnet, but its electrically operated port will not open. Every circuit is burned out.

You walk back to the dome. All is peaceful again—you cannot even find the place Pickens was firing at.

You and Pickens stand looking helplessly at each other. There is nothing you can do now but wait.

The End

You and Pickens return to the Cygnet and radio the *Aloha*. The captain tells you that Dr. Vivaldi has surveyed a large area in *Cygnet III* and has reported finding a monument covered with writing. The computer has analyzed the inscriptions.

"Now we know the meaning of the message our astronomers first detected in Hawaii," the captain tells you. "It means 'We are coming.' Friends, a wise race of beings has been living on this planet. Many of them have fled, and others are hiding underground and under the sea, because this solar system will soon be swept by particles of antimatter that will destroy all life on the surface, and perhaps will even destroy the planet itself. The place they are fleeing to is our own planet—Earth!"

A few hours later the *Aloha* is once again traveling through interstellar space, heading home. As you look out at the vast panorama of stars and galaxies, you wonder what will become of the third planet from Altair.

The End

At this moment, the ocean of the Third Planet seems a forbidding place. You suspect there is more to be lost than gained by staying in it. You blast off and return to the *Aloha* at top speed.

The captain is distressed to hear that Bluenose has been put out of action. He directs you to proceed on a new mission, exploring inland—this time taking Dr. Vivaldi with you.

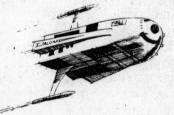

Turn to page 15.

As you explore an underwater ridge, a cluster of blobs approaches. You blast away with your laser weapon. The blobs frizzle and melt, dissolving into the surrounding water.

You continue on, following a long, curving formation of what looks like brown coral lying to the port side of your diving bubble. You glance to starboard and see a similar formation that was there a few moments before. Behind you is still another brown, curving form.

You activate the emergency ascent device. Your bubble rises rapidly—into the oily brown mass of a hungry blob.

The End

54

Since you can't save the captain and Dr. Vivaldi unless you save the *Aloha,* you and Pickens proceed toward Altair's tenth planet, the outermost one. From this position you should be able to safely monitor the whole Altair system.

By the time you reach the outer limits of the Altair system, many of the planets are surrounded by pink light. Tongues of flame leap from Altair's surface tens of millions of kilometers into space. You ask the computer for its analysis.

"ANTIMATTER ACTIVITY INCREASING. LIFE THREATENED ON ALL PLANETS EXCEPT NUMBER 6."

Why is the Sixth Planet escaping the antimatter storms? Could there be some natural cause for it, or is it the work of alien beings?

If you decide to wait for the time being on the edge of the Altair system, turn to page 74.

If you decide to investigate the Sixth Planet, turn to page 75.

You insert the chronistan program into the computer, which emits a musical tone that rises higher and higher until it becomes a searing pain shooting through your head. In a moment you are unconscious.

Some time later you awaken and look around. You and the three others are in another spaceship, larger and more comfortable than the *Aloha*. Through the enormous windows of this new ship you can see the whole galaxy.

"I can tell by the arrangement of the constellations that we have traveled a few thousand years in time," Pickens says.

Turn to page 57.

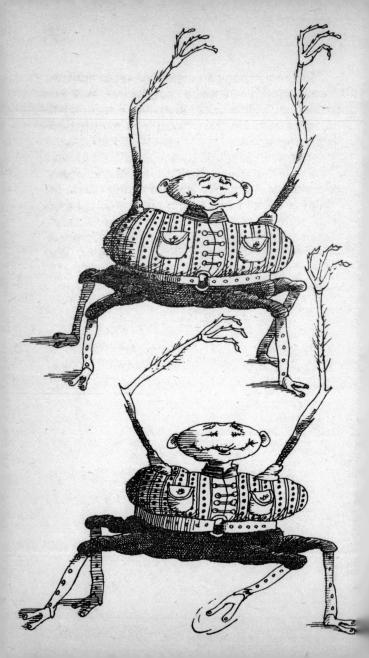

You are astounded to see that there are two strange creatures in the compartment. They have squat bodies, four legs, and oval heads. Each holds up ropelike arms and waves its spiny hands. You understand—they are welcoming you aboard *their* ship!

Within a few hours, you are able to establish communication with these beings through computer-assisted translation. They tell you that they come from the third planet from Altair and that their destination is the third planet from the Sun—the Earth! You will arrive in only a few weeks—you can only guess whether it will be in the future or the past.

The End

58

You realize that there is danger in remaining in orbit, but you do not wish to desert Dr. Vivaldi and the captain. You desperately keep trying to reach them by radio.

Suddenly, the *Aloha* is jolted by the most violent wave of antimatter activity yet. The ship's integrity alarm is sounding. "EMERGENCY ACTION REQUIRED," the computer says.

"We're losing altitude," Pickens reports.

"EXTRAORDINARY AIR TURBULENCE PROJECTED," the computer continues. "RECOMMEND SUBMERSION IN OCEAN."

"Submersion?" you say.

"The ship is theoretically able to submerge and maneuver to depths of up to ninety meters," Pickens says, "but this is recommended only in an extreme emergency."

The *Aloha* is now descending through the Third Planet's atmosphere, jolted out of its orbit by antimatter waves. You could bring it down on fairly smooth ground—or in the ocean.

"I think there's something wrong with the computer program for this situation," Pickens says. "I can't believe it has taken into account the high seas we are going to encounter."

If you land in the ocean and submerge,
turn to page 77.

If you set down on dry land, turn to page 78.

You sit on a rock and rest, relieved to have escaped from the giant rat beast. You close your eyes for a moment, but at once feel a presence behind you. You turn quickly and try to jump away—too late.

The End

You decide that the benefits of returning to your own time are not great enough to risk extinction. The *Aloha* will stay in its new time—for better or for worse.

After your initial shock wears off, you order the computer to analyze stellar positions. In a few minutes the computer reports, "PATTERNS OF STELLAR AND GALACTIC POSITIONS SHOW TIME ADVANCE 487 MILLION YEARS. STAR ALTAIR BEARS 87-22-18 DISTANCE -- ONE-HALF LIGHT-YEAR."

"It is a miracle that Altair's so close," Pickens says, "but look at the display screen—Altair has lost a lot of its mass."

"And four of its planets," Dr. Vivaldi adds. "The Third Planet is still there, but it is surrounded by an electromagnetic screen."

"There is a lot of antimatter in this solar system," Pickens goes on. "If we pass near any of it, we will be annihilated."

If you decide to enter Altair's planetary system, turn to page 62.

If not, turn to page 69.

The captain orders the computer to put the *Aloha* on course for Altair once again. Soon afterward, the computer reports that the ship has been deflected from its new heading and is passing dangerously close to a black hole—a collapsed star so dense that light cannot escape from its surface.

"Employ the full-propulsion booster," the captain says. The ship shifts course. The engines strain. A few minutes later, a warning light flashes on. The booster is exhausted. The computer reports that if you use utmost emergency force the ship can safely bypass the black hole, but its power reserve will then be nearly depleted and you will have to return directly to Earth. If you use only ordinary power, you will retain enough fuel to continue on to Altair—but there is a 40-percent chance that you will be pulled into the black hole.

The captain puts the question to a vote. Again, opinion is divided, and your vote will decide.

If you vote to try to make it past the black hole on ordinary power, turn to page 83.

If you vote to use all available energy to escape, turn to page 84.

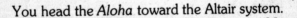

You head the *Aloha* toward the Altair system.

"Screen 25!" Pickens suddenly calls out. "Missile approaching from sector .035. Range less than a million kilometers."

You have no time to think. You quickly depress the buttons that activate the advance detonation devices. A computer screen flashes the vital information that in 3.7 seconds the oncoming missile will be detonated at a distance of three hundred fifty kilometers, and that the initial blast will reach the *Aloha* in one minute, two seconds. Another screen flashes, "DAMAGE PREDICTION -- 98-PERCENT CHANCE TOTAL DESTRUCTION."

Instantly you press the time-override acceleration alarm. Then you punch out computer instructions and adjust the blast resistors.

With a whining, grinding sound the *Aloha*
shudders and accelerates toward the space/time
vortex. Monitors show a brilliant orange cloud in
sector .035—all that remains of the missile.

You look at Pickens. He shakes his head. He
knows your question, and you know his answer.
There is no hope.

The End

64

The *Aloha* veers off and accelerates toward Caprion—the center of the expanding universe. Glorious harmonic sounds resonate through the ship. Your mind begins to fill with beautiful images. Through the forward port you see a point of dazzling blue light.

"This is a trap!" the captain cries out. "Full hyperspeed reverse!" But the ship does not respond. It is being pulled by an overwhelming force toward the blue light.

"It will be all right," Dr. Vivaldi says. "Somehow I know we can trust whatever is happening to us."

"DESTINATION POINT 1 MINUTE," the computer reports.

"Prepare to fire neutron destruct device directly at the blue light!" the captain calls out.

"DEVICE READY. DECISION TIME 8 SECONDS."

"Stop him from firing!" Dr. Vivaldi calls to you. "This is our chance to learn the secret of the universe!"

If you stop the captain from firing, turn to page 86.

If you do not, turn to page 89.

Fortunately, the people are friendly. They take you to their village, a cluster of rude shelters interspersed with huge stone monuments. To your surprise, you find Dr. Vivaldi in the village. She encountered some of the villagers while searching for you.

"Have you examined these monuments?" she asks excitedly. "They are exactly like the ones on Easter Island in the Pacific Ocean!"

You are aware that no one knows who fashioned the Easter Island monuments, or why.

After photographing the monuments, you return to your Cygnet in Dr. Vivaldi's shuttlecraft and ascend to the *Aloha*. The captain is amazed by your report.

Go on to the next page.

"I only wish we could investigate this planet further," he says. "But our medical sensors indicate that there are microorganisms in the atmosphere that we have no defenses against. If we stay here, we will become fatally ill."

The *Aloha* blasts out of stationary orbit and is soon streaking past Altair's outermost planet.

"If I am right," the captain says to you as the two of you are standing on the bridge, "we are not the first to have made the trip between Earth and the third planet from Altair."

The End

You stay hidden until the humanoid creatures have passed. By the time you make your way back to the Cygnet, flickering lights cover the sky. All your radio and radar equipment is burned out. You quickly blast off and almost immediately spot the *Aloha* overhead. You dock as quickly as possible.

"We never thought you'd make it," the captain tells you. "Fortunately, we were able to track you. We're hyping out immediately—antimatter storms may overwhelm this planet within hours. It is time for us to return home."

In a few minutes, the *Aloha* is speeding through space. Safe once more, you breathe a sigh of relief.

"Change course to Deneb 5," the captain commands you.

You are startled by the captain's behavior. There is no conceivable reason for going to Deneb 5.

You exchange glances with Dr. Vivaldi, who is standing next to you. "Watch the captain closely," she whispers. "I think he may be in the grip of an alien mind force."

Turn to page 12.

"I think it would be futile to try to pass the electromagnetic barriers," you tell the others. They nod in agreement. The *Aloha* whirls you into interstellar space at a time hundreds of millions of years in the future. Now you must search for a planet somewhere on which to start a new life, for it has been a long time since any radio signals were sent from the third planet from Altair—or anyone was listening on the planet Earth.

The End

You activate the chronistan. A terrible whining sound like that of a jet engine forces you to your knees in pain.

The next thing you feel is a dull headache. Rubbing your eyes, you quickly call up a display of the Altair system on one of the computer screens. Everything is calm. There are no flashes of light.

You think that everything has worked out all right, and then you realize that the *Aloha* is drifting in space. You find that the ship's neutron drive is irreparably damaged.

Go on to the next page.

On the Third Planet, the captain and Dr. Vivaldi will be waiting for you; their survival supplies will not last indefinitely. You could reach the Third Planet in a few days, but that would mean using up every ounce of your retro-rocket fuel. What if you don't have quite enough to make it? It might be wiser to wait a month until the planet passes close by—that way you could make it with fuel to spare.

If you proceed to the Third Planet at once, turn to page 106.

If you wait, turn to page 107.

The aliens do not speak again. Soon orange, shimmering lights begin to race about your brain. You realize that you are going to black out. Suddenly, the *Aloha* is violently wrenched from its orbit by an overwhelming force.

Then it seems to be perfectly still in space, while galaxies hurtle by and stars explode, bursting like skyrockets, shedding white sparks against the blackness of space.

You look at Pickens. His face is filled with horror. "The aliens are dragging us not through space, but through time—to their time," he says.

"Look at the data analysis screen," you say. "The galaxies are moving closer together. That means the universe has stopped expanding. It is now contracting. We must be very, very far in the future."

"Yes, but look at screen 8," Pickens replies. "We are very close to a solar system like our own."

You manipulate the computer's controls. In a few moments, you get this report: "THERE IS A 15-PERCENT CHANCE OF RETURNING TO EARTH TIME BY ACTIVATING THE CHRONISTAN. FAILURE WOULD MEAN INSTANT ANNIHILATION."

If you try to return from the future by activating the chronistan, turn to page 108.

If you wait to see if you can find a less risky way to return to Earth time/space, turn to page 111.

You assume stationary orbit at the outer edge of the Altair system, where you can safely await developments. As you watch the display screen, you are startled to see Altair beginning to lose part of its spectrum. Pulsating waves of light fly out from its surface. Then sensors show that its first and fifth planets have disappeared!

You ask the computer for an analysis, but there is no response. Everything is oddly quiet. Eerie flickering lights dance about the instruments on the bridge.

Pickens says he'll try to de-energize all computer functions except those necessary to hype the *Aloha* out of the Altair system. He looks up, intending to ask you to help, but you are no longer there.

The End

The *Aloha* speeds toward the Sixth Planet, a mysterious sphere only half the size of Earth. As you approach, all sensors are deployed to detect any unusual electromagnetic effect.

"PLANET 6 ANALYZED. DATA SHOWS ANTIGRAVITY EFFECT CONTRARY TO KNOWN LAWS OF PHYSICS," the computer reports.

Suddenly, some force takes hold of the ship, locking it into orbit around the Sixth Planet. You are unable to get back on course. Your only chance of escaping is to activate your time-override acceleration device—a procedure that might rip the *Aloha* apart.

If you activate the TOA device, turn to page 91.

If you do not, turn to page 92.

You bring the *Aloha* down onto the ocean surface. The ship is badly jolted by the high waves. You immediately press the emergency descent button. In a moment the ship submerges and comes to rest on the ocean floor, only a few meters above maximum safe depth. You and Pickens breathe a sigh of relief when you find that it has escaped damage.

You launch Bluenose, your underwater robot, to investigate the surrounding area and to check conditions on the surface. An hour later, it transmits sonar pictures that are displayed on a computer screen. The *Aloha* is not far from a large dome set in a rock ledge. The dome is made of extremely hard crystalline material.

An atmospheric probe reveals that the antimatter storms have subsided. For the moment, at least, it would be safe to surface and start a search for the captain and Dr. Vivaldi.

"That dome could be the roof of an underwater city," Pickens says. "And such a city might be the source of the signals we've come so far to trace!"

If you bring the Aloha *up to the surface while you have a chance, turn to page 80.*

If you decide to investigate the crystal dome, turn to page 82.

You are about to set down on the beach when the *Aloha* is engulfed by showers of sparks. You instruct the computer to execute an emergency blast-off.

The ship shudders; you hear a whirring sound that rises in pitch. The amber and purple emergency stress lights are flashing.

"CRITICAL DANGER. COMPUTER ASSISTANCE IMPOSSIBLE BECAUSE UNKNOWN FORCE IS OVERRIDING COMPUTER FUNCTIONS."

As the computer speaks, you feel yourself losing consciousness. In a moment you are asleep and dreaming—dreaming of the *Aloha* stretching in distorted space/time, traveling at such speed that billions of galaxies fly by on either side, above and below. And then you seem to be leaving the universe itself.

But is all this a dream? Or is it reality? You sit up and call out to Pickens. In a shaky voice he reports having had the same experience you had.

Through the windows you can see an array of stars unlike any you have ever seen before. Either you are still dreaming, or you are awake in another universe.

The End

The computer makes more sounds, as if in reply. You talk to it some more. It answers—this time repeating some English words you used. You realize that the computer is learning your language! Within half an hour it is communicating in broken English. It tells you that within its memory banks is all knowledge ever attained by the inhabitants of the Third Planet.

Soon afterward the *Aloha* returns. The captain, Pickens, and Dr. Vivaldi are excited by your discovery. But they report that antibiotics brought from Earth are proving very ineffective against dangerous microorganisms in the atmosphere of the Third Planet. The ship must leave immediately or you will all become fatally ill.

Although the computer is too bulky to load aboard the *Aloha,* Pickens is able to detach some of its memory banks and bring them along.

"We have not completed our mission," the captain says. "But with the knowledge of the Third Planet's people stored in these memory banks, we may be able to do much for the peoples of the Earth."

The End

On the surface, you manage to reach Dr. Vivaldi and the captain by radio. They have been searching for you in the Cygnet. They come aboard just as the computer is warning that another violent antimatter storm is approaching. Several of Altair's planets are surrounded by flickering lights. The sun-star Altair is pulsating wildly.

"There is no choice," the captain says. "Hyper-takeoff, ten seconds." In a few minutes, the *Aloha* is streaking through interstellar space.

"We must analyze this solar system from a safe distance—" the captain begins.

"Captain!" Pickens calls out. "We have detected an unusual object five billion kilometers away, bearing 35-22-16."

At the speed at which the *Aloha* is traveling, the object is incredibly close. The captain orders the slight change of course needed to reach it.

"Decelerate from hyperspeed," he orders.

Within a few hours you are alongside the object. It is in the shape of a perfect sphere—clearly the creation of intelligent beings. Your sensors detect no sign of life, no radioactivity, no electronic emanations, nothing.

The captain asks you to take a "space walk" to examine the exterior of the object.

Turn to page 110.

As you prepare to investigate the crystal dome, you receive radio signals from the captain and Dr. Vivaldi. They are preparing to submerge and come aboard the *Aloha*. A few minutes later you welcome them back and tell them what you have planned.

"Proceed to the dome," the captain orders.

Soon the *Aloha* rests poised in the water a few feet above the blue crystal dome.

"Sensor data show that the dome is made of materials harder than any known on Earth," Pickens reports.

"Supermatter," says the captain. "But I'm sure we can penetrate it with our neutron laser."

"Wait!" says Dr. Vivaldi. "If the dome *is* part of a city, surely we should try to send the inhabitants a message of friendship before we do anything else. Let's send the same signals we were receiving from the planet when we started out."

"I don't think we have time," the captain says. "It may only be safe to surface and leave this planet for a short while longer. And, if there *are* beings in that dome, they may very well be hostile. It would be better to take them by surprise. I think we should start to drill at once. Do you agree?" he asks you.

If you advise drilling at once,
turn to page 93.

If you advise sending the signals,
turn to page 94.

The computer plots the optimum course for avoiding the black hole. In a few minutes it shows that your probability of making it past the black hole is increasing—62.3 percent, 68.1 percent, 71 percent. Everyone is greatly relieved. But suddenly the critical-data light begins flashing and the computer reports, "BLACK HOLE HAS CONSUMED A SMALLER BLACK HOLE. MASS INCREASE 18.6 PERCENT."

"What probability now?" the captain asks.

"PROBABILITY OF ESCAPE IS ZERO."

You look out at the black disc in the sky; it is obscuring more and more stars as it looms larger and larger. Within a few minutes, it covers an area as big as the constellation Orion.

"There is a chance," Dr. Vivaldi says. "We could pass safely through the black hole and into another universe."

"Very unlikely," Pickens replies.

The End

By using all available energy in one thrust, the *Aloha* escapes from the pull of the black hole.

A few weeks later, you land safely on Earth. Although you were unable to reach Altair and find out who was sending the signals, or what they meant, you have learned a great deal about the problems and perils of interstellar space travel.

At a United Nations ceremony, you and the other members of the crew are honored with the "Ambassador of the Planet Earth" award—a gold medal bearing the inscription PEACE ON EARTH, PEACE FROM EARTH, PEACE TO EARTH.

The End

You continue on. Soon you come to what sems to be a spaceship. It is half the size of the *Aloha,* and every part of it appears to be made of crystal. A door opens and you cautiously enter.

Within a few moments lights flash on and you hear the hum of electronic equipment. A display screen lights up. You and Dr. Vivaldi watch in amazement as a movie begins on the screen. First it shows Altair and its planets; then a close-up of the third planet; then the camera sweeps across the planet's surface. Flashing lights grow brighter and brighter on the screen until they hurt your eyes. Then the film shows dozens of spaceships taking off, then a shot of the cave, then a single ship flying out of the cave and into space, and finally a diagram of a star surrounded by planets. The movie ends. The screen flashes a mass of twelve dots, then eleven, then ten, then nine. . . .

"This ship is going to take off," Dr. Vivaldi says, "and if we don't get out right now, it will take off with us in it!"

You start to head for the door, but Dr. Vivaldi grabs your arm. "We are explorers," she says. "We may find out a great deal more by staying on this ship than by leaving it."

If you stay aboard, turn to page 88.

If you leave the ship, turn to page 103.

You insert your special safeguard code key into the computer, thus preventing it from firing the neutron destruct device.

"This is mutiny!" the captain screams at you. But his words are lost in a thundering musical chord.

In a moment, you are in darkness. All is quiet; yet some living presence is thinking with your brain! Somehow you know you are at the beginning of time—that you are a spirit that exists in the universe and someday will inhabit a person on Earth. First you will be asleep for billions of years, but your awakening will seem to come only an instant later—in fact, right now.

The End

Within a few minutes the crystal ship is heading toward outer space. You signal the *Aloha*. The captain radios that the *Aloha* will follow the crystal ship.

"EMERGENCY!" the ship's display screen flashes. "ACTIVATE HYPERTIME DRIVE!" The next thing you know, Altair is so far away it looks like any other bright star. There is a printout on the screen: "HYPERTIME DRIVE DESTROYED BY ANTIMATTER STORM. TIME TO NEW PLANET 650 YEARS. HUMAN LIFE SPAN INSUFFICIENT FOR VOYAGE."

"How will we survive?" you ask.

"HIBERNATION CHAMBER AVAILABLE. SURVIVAL CHANCES FOR ALANIAN TRAVELERS 99.7 PERCENT. FOR HUMANS INSUFFICIENT DATA. DELAY IN HIBERNATION DECREASES CHANCES FOR SURVIVAL."

"The Alanians," you say. "They must be the people who built this ship."

Dr. Vivaldi decides to try hibernation. She enters the chamber and in a few minutes seems to be sleeping peacefully. You are tempted to follow, but there is no sign of the *Aloha*, and you are anxious to learn whether it survived the antimatter storm. If it did, and you can make contact, perhaps it can rescue you.

If you try to contact the Aloha,
turn to page 112.

*If you enter the hibernation chamber,
turn to page 116.*

The computer fires one of the *Aloha*'s neutron destruct devices. But the *Aloha* itself is now traveling at time-override acceleration. In a moment it overtakes its own neutroid. The ship explodes silently as it enters the great blue light.

The End

You return to the door. Dr. Vivaldi presses against it firmly and it swings open. You see before you an enormous room, completely white, filled with electronic equipment.

"No sign of life—just an automatic control center of some kind," Dr. Vivaldi says as you walk along past banks of machines the purpose of which you can only guess at.

Suddenly, Dr. Vivaldi stumbles and falls. She cannot get up. She looks very pale. You begin to feel dizzy yourself. Dr. Vivaldi looks up at you. "Radiation?" she asks.

"I've already checked it," you reply.

"Do a microorganism scan."

You are shaking and are barely able to set up your scanner. Too weak to stand up any longer, you sit down beside Dr. Vivaldi. Together you examine the data.

"Ah, here it is," Dr. Vivaldi says in a feeble voice. "There are bacteria here of a type unknown on Earth. Their purpose is to protect this equipment from mold, insects, rats . . . fungi . . . from anything that might interfere . . . including alien creatures like you and me."

Dr. Vivaldi falls unconscious, and, in a moment, so do you.

The End

The moment you activate the TOA device you fall unconscious. When you come to, you check the display screens and are shocked to see that Altair is so far away that it looks like just another bright star. Pickens is lying at one end of the compartment. He is badly bruised, but otherwise unharmed.

The *Aloha* is virtually crippled, limited to travel at sublight speeds. It will take at least two years for you to return to the Altair system on neutron drive. Fortunately, you have on board the means to grow enough food to last you for several years. Whether the captain and Dr. Vivaldi can survive until you arrive—if you arrive—only time will tell.

The End

You are not willing to risk trying the *Aloha*'s TOA device. Instead, you and Pickens study the situation in hopes of finding some mode of escape. But you have little time to think, for in a few minutes the amber and purple stress lights begin to flash. The computer begins an emergency printout: "UNAUTHORIZED PERSON SCANNING MY MEMORY BANKS." You know an alien life form must be present.

Suddenly, the computer starts talking—but it is not the computer, it is the alien speaking through the computer. "WE KNOW ALL ABOUT YOU. WE ARE TAKING THIS PLANET THROUGH A TIME/SPACE SINGULARITY INTO OUR UNIVERSE. IF YOU FOLLOW INSTRUCTIONS YOU WILL COME TOO. OTHERWISE YOU WILL DIE. YOUR FIRST INSTRUCTION IS TO SAY NOTHING."

If you obey the alien's order and say nothing, turn to page 97.

If you tell the aliens they have no right to abduct you, turn to page 98.

If you try to convince the aliens that you come in friendship, turn to page 102.

The captain immediately activates the neutron laser. A flashing green light on the control panel is the only indication that the beam is drilling into the crystal dome.

Suddenly, your hair stands on end. Sparks are flying everywhere. You reach for the emergency stop-function button, but you are sent reeling by a violent shock. Moments later, all that remains of the *Aloha* is a puff of smoke rising from the ocean.

The End

"All right, try your signals," the captain tells Dr. Vivaldi.

It takes only a moment for the computer to select the famous signals from its memory banks and broadcast them through the dome, and it is only a moment more before the same signals are received on the *Aloha*. Everyone cheers.

The captain immediately orders the computer to begin exchanging language information with the beings in the dome. In only a few minutes the computer is able to understand some of the alien language.

Dr. Vivaldi analyzes the computer's crude translation. "I'm not sure I understand their message," she says, "but I think they are defending themselves against antimatter storms. They can open up their dome and let the *Aloha* enter, but, if antimatter activity grows stronger, they may not be able to let us out."

Go on to the next page.

The captain says he would like his crew to make the decision. Dr. Vivaldi favors entering the dome, but Pickens is opposed.

Your vote will decide.

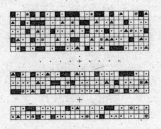

*If you vote to enter the dome,
turn to page 99.*

If you do not, turn to page 100.

Feeling you have no choice, you remain silent. If you can just stay alive, at least you can have hope of returning someday to your own universe.

Several minutes pass and you begin to wonder whether you may be dreaming. Then, suddenly, you feel what seems to be an electric shock. You try to cry out to Pickens, but find that you cannot speak. You sit paralyzed, surrounded by shimmering, dancing lights. . . .

Now you find yourself free to move again, but you are face to face with a thin, wiry creature with a large round head from which dozens of long spikes protrude. Speaking a language that you have never heard before, but that you somehow can understand perfectly, the creature says, "Welcome. I am sure you will enjoy your new world . . . *if you will just obey orders.*"

The End

"Surely it is wrong in your universe, as it is in ours, to enslave another being. Let us go!" you cry out.

The voice is silent, and you thankfully note that you are still alive.

"I think you have confused this alien mind," Pickens says. "For the moment it does not seem to be able to act."

"And we still control the computer," you say. "Computer, what did you learn from the aliens while they were scanning your memory banks?"

"THEY ARE AFRAID OF OUR CHRONISTAN. THEY INSTRUCTED ME TO DESTROY IT BUT MY OWN SECURITY PROGRAM PREVENTED ME FROM DOING SO."

"Suppose, computer," you say, "we activate our chronistan?"

"WE WILL BE THROWN AT LEAST A YEAR INTO THE PAST. THIS WILL DESTROY OUR TIME-CONTRACTION DEVICE. CAUTION—33-PERCENT CHANCE OF VAPORIZING ALOHA," the computer replies.

You realize that if you could hurl the *Aloha* a year into the past, it would ensure your escape from the alien beings and give you the time you need to rescue the captain and Dr. Vivaldi.

If you try it, turn to page 70.

If you do not, turn to page 72.

The decision made, Dr. Vivaldi orders the computer to trasmit the message "We desire to enter." You watch the sensor-information display panel. In a few minutes, your computer analysis appears: "DOME ROTATING AT 8 DEGREES PER MINUTE."

You realize that the dome is actually a sphere. A few minutes later its underside faces you, and an entire quadrant slides open. The *Aloha* is drawn within and the opened section slides closed.

The display screen shows that you are in a cavern several kilometers across. The ground is covered with blue-green moss. Groves of tall, feathery plants, colored as brightly as tropical fish, bedeck the landscape. Not far from the *Aloha* are groups of crystal cubes, each as big as a small room, stacked one on top of another and set back at each level like the steps of a pyramid.

Looking through the windows into the gloom of the cavern, you see a single gray figure, about four feet in height, emerge from one of the crystal cubes and slowly move toward the *Aloha*. Its perfectly round head sits on a squat body supported by four flexible legs. It holds two long spindly arms aloft, waving them as if they were antennae.

Turn to page 105.

Much as you would like to meet the Third Planet's inhabitants, you are unwilling to risk having to stay in the dome forever. After you make a final sensor sweep of conditions on the surface of the planet, the *Aloha* ascends, breaks through the waves, and blasts into orbit.

"The time has come for us to leave," the captain says. "Scientific research must discover a shield against antimatter storms. Only then can we return to the third planet from Altair."

The End

As you continue on into the cave, Dr. Vivaldi suddenly grabs your arm.

"Look . . . the floor has been smoothed out along a wide strip, as if for a roadway," she says. "And look back there, on your right—see those cracks on that smooth wall? I think that is a door!"

"And look up ahead," you say. "Cave art!" The walls are covered with drawings of strange creatures unlike any you have ever seen.

"Extraordinary," Dr. Vivaldi says. "Shall we continue on, or go back and try to open that door?"

If you say, "Let's continue on,"
turn to page 85.

If you say, "Let's try the door,"
turn to page 90.

"Please give us a moment," you say. "We come in friendship. Make yourselves known to us. We have much to learn from each other."

Suddenly, a dense fog fills the compartment. In a moment, it clears. You rush to the controls and, to your joy, find that the *Aloha* has been freed from its orbit around the Sixth Planet. And the interfering aliens have simply vanished.

You immediately set course for the Third Planet. Your sensors locate *Cygnet I,* waiting for you in orbit, and in a few hours you are reunited with the captain and Dr. Vivaldi.

They are astonished to hear of your encounter with the aliens.

"There is no question you were present when and where space/time of our universe touched space/time of another universe," the captain says.

"How many universes can there be?" you wonder aloud.

"Before this happened, I would have said one," Pickens muses. "Now, I believe the number is infinite."

The End

You leave the crystal ship, and, after a moment's hesitation, Dr. Vivaldi follows you. The ship's door shuts behind you. Somehow you know it will not open for you again.

"Follow me," Dr. Vivaldi says. "Perhaps there are life forms nearby."

You follow her deeper into the cavern, and finally enter a tunnel that winds upward to the surface. You have not met any beings—you have only sensed their presence.

The land outside the cave is barren and strewn with boulders. The sky is filled with red-orange light. The sun-star Altair is hidden behind a bank of gray clouds. You fire an emergency/distress rocket, and then another. In less than an hour *Cygnet II* coasts in to a landing.

Soon you are safely back on the *Aloha*. The captain listens to your story. Then he tells you that, just before your return, the computer tracked a spaceship leaving the planet.

In a few minutes the *Aloha* leaves orbit in pursuit of the ship. Your visit to the third planet from Altair has ended, and a new quest is beginning.

The End

The hours stretch into days; the days stretch into weeks. Now you have waited so long that the computer tells you your chances of surviving hibernation are nearly zero. You can only hope that somehow your crystal ship will reach the new planet before you grow old and die, or that you will at last find the *Aloha,* or that something will happen to fix the ship's hypertime device. But the months go by and nothing changes. You grow more and more depressed as you sit and wait, and finally, disoriented by the incredible loneliness of outer space, you lose all will to survive.

The End

When the creature reaches the *Aloha*, the captain hesitates a moment and then opens the port and beckons it inside. Your sensors show that it talks by making ultrasonic vibrations, sounds too high for human beings to hear, but, with the help of the computer, Dr. Vivaldi is able to converse with it. She tells you the creature is an Alanian.

Through her, you learn that the Alanians have been forced to live under the ocean in order to protect themselves against antimatter storms. A new storm will soon strike, and they fear that the whole planet may be annihilated. Even if their shield is effective, they will not dare open the portal for many months. If the *Aloha* is to leave, it must leave at once.

The captain decides that the *Aloha* must depart, but he asks if you would volunteer to stay on as a kind of ambassador. "I wouldn't ask you," he says, "except that we have less than a 20-percent chance of making it out of the Altair system. If we all die, our mission will have been in vain. But if you stay here, you will probably survive—and you may someday find a way of uniting the people of our two planets."

If you say you'll stay, turn to page 113.

If you say you want to leave with the others, turn to page 114.

You immediately plot a course to the Third Planet and fire your retro-rockets, causing the *Aloha* to slowly accelerate and head for the place in space where the Third Planet will be in four days.

Now that antimatter interference has been removed, radio communication is possible. You soon reach Dr. Vivaldi and the captain. They took refuge in a cave during the antimatter storm; they report that they have found good sources of food, but no signs of intelligent life.

Four days later, as you approach the Third Planet, the *Aloha* is caught in the gravitational field of the water moon. In plotting your course, the computer did not compensate for this. You try to escape the moon's gravitational pull without exhausting your fuel supply, but you are forced to apply additional power. Within a few moments the instruments reveal that you are out of fuel.

You activate an emergency booster rocket. It is not enough. You are falling, faster and faster. . . .

SPLASH!

The End

You and Pickens settle down to wait for the Third Planet to reach its closest point of approach. You are able to contact Dr. Vivaldi and the captain by radio; they have survived the antimatter storm. For the moment, all is calm on the Third Planet.

It is a month before you and Pickens fire your retro-rockets and glide into stationary orbit above the Cygnet, which soon afterward blasts off and maneuvers alongside. The crew is finally reunited.

"There is plenty of food for us on this planet," the captain says.

"Thank goodness for that," you reply. "Now that the neutron drive is out of commission, the *Aloha* is able to travel only by conventional nuclear power. Our top speed is barely ninety-six million kilometers per hour."

"At that rate," Pickens says, "we would reach Earth in one hundred eighty years."

"We are no longer visitors," muses Dr. Vivaldi. "The third planet from Altair is now our home."

The End

You activate the chronistan and instantly become unconscious.

When you awaken, the rapid movement of the galaxy has stopped. Time is once again progressing at a normal rate. But Pickens is dead. The violent transposition of space/time was too great a strain on his heart. You bury him in the eternal reaches of space and say a prayer.

You are all alone, but your spirits are lifted by the very bright star shining through the starboard windows—it is so close by that you can see three of its planets.

The *Aloha* is partly crippled, but you are able to make your way toward the nearby solar system at reduced speed. Your sensors show that the star's third planet is apparently habitable.

Three weeks later you are able to crash-land the *Aloha* in this new world—one that is filled with hills and forests, lakes and streams that remind you of those on Earth.

By foraging about you, you find all the food you need. During the ensuing months, you explore much of the planet. Though it abounds in strange and wonderful animals, higher life forms apparently have not yet evolved. You believe that someday they will, and that someone will discover that you were here before them.

The End

You quickly surface. The blobs are repulsive to you, but their ability to join into one organism fascinates you. Could they be an intelligent life form? The data you have collected should be analyzed right away by the sophisticated computer on the *Aloha*. You return to the Cygnet and radio the captain that you are returning to the ship.

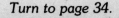

Turn to page 34.

Wearing tiny rockets that will permit you to maneuver, you step out into space. The sphere appears to be made of incredibly hard ceramic material. You apply your laser torch, but it won't even scratch the surface.

Then, to your astonishment, a large hatch slides open. You slip inside and a moving floor takes you into what seems to be the main chamber of the sphere.

In the center of the chamber are five transparent cubicles. Each of them contains a sleeping humanoid about one meter tall.

You report back to the *Aloha* by radio.

"They are probably programmed to wake up at a certain time. It would be dangerous to interfere," Dr. Vivaldi says.

You take photographs, make electronic copies of the ship's memory banks, and return to the *Aloha.*

While you are studying the data you've gathered, the captain announces, "Computer analysis shows that our energy resources have been drained. We must return to Earth immediately."

"We did not succeed in our mission," Dr. Vivaldi says, "but we certainly found intelligent life in space."

"Somehow," Pickens remarks, "I will never feel lonely again."

The End

You can't bring yourself to take a 15-percent chance. But you and Pickens and the computer fail to devise a better escape mode. Wearily you turn to the windows and gaze out.

For what seems like only a few minutes, you watch the sky growing brighter and brighter as the stars and galaxies fall toward a common center.

Soon the sky around you is almost a sheet of white light. The temperature is rising rapidly.

"We are about to have the singular experience," says Pickens, "of being present at the end of our universe."

"And perhaps," you reply, "at the beginning of the next one."

The End

112

You desperately try to locate the *Aloha* with the crystal ship's radio telescope. Meanwhile, the ship's computer provides you with information about life on the third planet from Altair. You learn that the crystal ship was indeed built by the Alanians, who were the gifted inhabitants of the Third Planet. They lived on the land, under the sea, and even in a city in the sky. Years ago they discovered that antimatter might annihilate Altair and all its planets, so they left the Altair system in their crystal ships.

In a few hours, the computer has told you everything you could want to know about the Third Planet. Now there is little for you to do but look out at the stars and continue to monitor the radio telescope.

Dr. Vivaldi is still sleeping peacefully, and you begin to think more and more about entering the hibernation chamber. The computer, when consulted about hibernation, will only tell you that to maximize your chances of survival, you must enter the chamber immediately. Yet you feel that if you wait just a little while longer, you will surely locate the *Aloha*.

If you keep trying to contact the Aloha, turn to page 104.

If you enter the hibernation chamber, turn to page 116.

There is no time for farewells. In a moment, the sphere rotates, the door slides open, and the *Aloha* is released into the ocean.

You have never felt so homesick in your life, but your hosts do their best to make you comfortable. They teach you thought transference without language. And they tell you their history.

You learn that some inhabitants of the Third Planet set up underground shelters where they hoped to survive the antimatter storms and learn how to combat them. Others fled in spaceships to find refuge elsewhere in the universe. Before the spaceships left, the Alanians searched the galaxies with enormous telescopes until they found the best possible planet to colonize. Then, while they were preparing for the long journey, they sent a message to that planet, the meaning of which was, "We are coming."

The End

You and the other crew members touch the Alanian's hands in a gesture of farewell. Then this strange and wonderful creature bows and departs into the amber gloom. The sphere rotates, the sliding door opens, and a few minutes later the *Aloha* surfaces on the ocean of the Third Planet.

"Blast off into orbit," the captain orders.

As the *Aloha* rises through the atmosphere, the planet seems bathed in flickering orange lights. A huge cloud of steam surrounds the water moon. The *Aloha* swerves violently from its course.

"Execute emergency hyperescape course!" the captain calls out.

The *Aloha* wrenches itself out of the Third Planet's gravitational field and streaks into space.

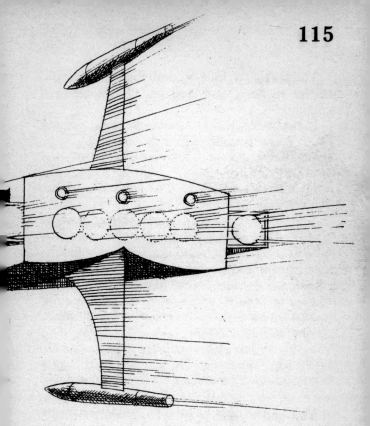

A few hours later, the ship is stabilized on hyperspeed and headed for Earth.

"We have not completed our mission, but we shall return to the third planet from Altair," the captain says.

"There may not be anything to return to," Pickens replies.

The End

You take a last look around, thank the computer for its help, and step into the hibernation chamber. . . .

Sunlight floods through the windows of your ship. You rub your eyes and stretch, trying to remember where you are and when it is—and even who you are. . . . The sun here is not the superbrilliant white disc of Altair. It looks more like Earth's sun.

You notice a familiar figure looking down at you. It is Dr. Vivaldi. She helps you out of the hibernation chamber, and you wander about the ship peering out the windows at your new surroundings. A fresh breeze blows in. A bird that looks like a blue jay flies by. You see a small animal running along the ground. It looks like a chipmunk!

"I'm very happy that you are awake," Dr. Vivaldi says. "We are on the new planet. The computer was badly damaged when we landed. So we're on our own—somewhere, sometime."

You hardly hear what she is saying, because you are lost in thought—staring at a crumpled tin can on the ground on which you can clearly see the words COCA-COLA.

The End

ABOUT THE AUTHOR

A graduate of Princeton University and Columbia Law School, EDWARD PACKARD lives in New York City, where he is a practicing lawyer. Mr. Packard conceived of the idea for the Choose Your Own Adventure™ series in the course of telling bedtime stories to his children, Caroline, Andrea, and Wells.

ABOUT THE ILLUSTRATOR

PAUL GRANGER is a prize-winning illustrator and painter.

CHOOSE YOUR OWN ADVENTURE

You'll want all the books in the exciting *Choose Your Own Adventure* series offering you hundreds of fantasy adventures without ever leaving your chair. Each book takes you through an adventure—under the sea, in a space colony, on a volcanic island—in which you become the main character. What happens next in the story depends on the choices *you* make and *only you c*an decide how the story ends!